Simultaneous Times

Simultaneous Times

Vol. 1

SPACE COWBOY BOOKS

SPACE COWBOY BOOKS
61871 Twentynine Palms Hwy
Joshua Tree CA 92252
www.spacecowboybooks.com

Simultaneous Times Anthology Vol. 1
ISBN #978-1-7328257-0-3

First Edition | 2018
Cover Art and Illustrations by Zara Kand
Book design by Jon Christopher

CONTENTS

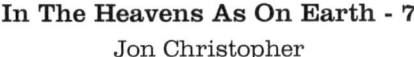

In The Heavens
As On Earth

———●———

Jon Christopher

Jeremy couldn't stop thinking about the dust balls in the hallways. The dust balls, the grimy fingerprints on the wall panels, the smeary view monitors – it seemed like no one cleaned anymore. *Maybe everybody is as sick of this place as I am,* thought Jeremy. He looked down at his nearly finished drink and nodded towards the bartender for a fresh one.

Jeremy stared out over the snaking landmass of Central America and toward the North American deserts in the disappearing horizon. There was a dusty smudge near the top corner of the view window distracting him from an extremely beautiful vantage point 220 miles above the surface of the planet. The view was lost on Jeremy this afternoon. He didn't even hear the background music that was ever-present on E.S. All he heard was the groaning and creaking of the massive station. Nobody else heard it unless they paid close attention, but Jeremy did. As a middle-management supervisor of the Station Services Corporation he had become attuned to the creaks and groans of the Equatorial Station - the mammoth ring that encircled the planet along the equatorial plane. It was his job to know the sounds of the station, at least in the Leo sub-section.

Jeremy had eight months left to go on his

second five-year contract. Upper management was already pressuring him to sign-up for another five years. This was one of the reasons he was sitting here in his favorite bar instead of working. No one else was around to distract him from his thoughts, just him and the bartender, a robotic presence that stayed out of the way and brought him fresh drinks when he nodded his head in its direction.

Jeremy's suit was well tailored and freshly pressed. His shirt had his initials monogrammed on the cuffs. His shoes had been shined that morning. Everything about him was in place, clean and with a natural air of elite superiority. He had a way of making people feel uncomfortable in his presence, and that could be because he didn't really like anyone. People were slobs who didn't care about the important things, like doing a good job, craftsmanship, using quality materials, and cleanliness.

Nine years of inspecting half-assed repairs around the E.S. had taken its toll. Where other people saw one of the greatest wonders of human engineering, Jeremy saw an aging, jerry-rigged, crippled monster on the verge of collapse. He hated the E.S. more than he hated being around people. Part way through his next drink he started to think about the desert again. When the next eight months were done and his contract was completed, he was going to leave this place, get back down on the surface, and move out to the desert. Maybe get a dog or something.

Twelve years before Jeremy was born, the Equatorial Station was completed. Gravity Lift Technology had been the key advancement that made the station possible. Once the ability to overcome the effects of gravity in small areas became a possibility, the door was opened to realize some of the futuristic dreams of the 20th century, like gravity elevators.

Gravity elevators had led to the development of geostationary space platforms 220 miles above the planet. Within a few years of building the first gravity elevator shipping center in Ecuador, nearly a dozen lifts had been built along the equator, including several in the middle of the Pacific Ocean on deep-water platforms. The deep-water platforms quickly became giant artificial islands and shipping ports.

Seven years after the first gravity elevator was erected, the International Community of Nations (I.C.N.), the newly formed world-wide governing body that had replaced the United Nations, decided to build the Equatorial Station (E.S.). A space platform 220 miles above the Earth that completely encircled the planet was an extremely ambitious project, originally envisioned as a giant space laboratory dedicated to the "betterment of humanity through science and international cooperation". High and lofty words for what turned out to be a resort for the elite, and a tax-haven for corporations and the super-rich. Some things never change.

The earliest incarnation of the E.S. was a giant enclosed bridge that surrounded the planet, connected with enormous tethers to a network of gravity lift stations. The gravity lifts were huge elevators that moved materials and people from the surface up to the station. They stopped at the lift stations of the E.S. on their way to space mining colonies 22,000 miles out from the Earth at the end of the tethers.

During the first few years of the E.S. they held a "Race Around The Globe" car race. This event galvanized the attention of the world every August, as the best drivers in the world drove the nearly 20,000 mile route from the prime meridian in their "non-polluting" race cars. They raced completely around the Earth and finished several days later back at the prime meridian. Back then the station had been new and exciting. But nothing stays that way; everything ages and so had the station.

In 2045 the International Community of Nations moved from the old U.N. building in New York to the E.S. Shortly after that, construction contracts written years earlier deeded large segments of the station to the seven multinationals that had built the station. New "business friendly" construction rules were written for the E.S., and immediately a building spree began that continued for years, until the E.S. became an over-grown behemoth by 2085.

To put it succinctly, the E.S. was an over-built, densely packed world-surrounding city with various parks interspersed between the sections of the city. The complete circle was divided into twelve segments, each one named after a sign in the zodiac. The Leo section, where Jeremy worked and lived, was a segment that started at the Ecuador Lift Station and continued westward through two time zones into the Pacific Ocean, close to the North American Alliance Lift Station.

If you weren't a contracted employee of Station Services, a part of the massive I.C.N. complex, an employee of one of the seven multinationals, or one of the super-rich elite families, you would probably never set foot on the station. The common person was neither wanted here nor was there any reason for them to be here. Everyone understood that pretty clearly. Jeremy liked it that way, or at least he used to. He wasn't so sure anymore. Especially when he thought about giving all this up and moving back down to the planet. *Being a common person might not be so bad,* Jeremy thought after downing the last of his fourth drink. He nodded towards the bartender for a fresh one, while he unbuttoned the top button on his shirt and loosened his tie.

Of course Jeremy had never been a common person, had no idea how to be a common person, or even what that entailed. But he was rapidly leaving the realm of rational thought, the alcohol was starting to have its way with him. He stared for a while out the view window, at the twilight descending across North America, his mind dreaming about a little desert home somewhere out near Joshua Tree in Southern California. He no longer noticed the dust up in the corner of the window that had been so distracting just a short while earlier.

———●———

At the home of a member of the "Bring Down The Ring Coalition of Joshua Tree," about a dozen people met over coffee and donuts. Like many other BDTRC groups around the world, this was another local gathering of people with hearts in the right place, but vastly outmatched by International Security and Intelligence (I.S.I.). Three of their fifteen members were covert agents of the I.S.I. One of those three happened to be the de-facto leader of the Joshua Tree chapter of BDTRC – Terry Grimes.

Terry was always the most outspoken member of the group to advocate the use of violent means to bring down the E.S. Other members were in favor of using legitimate means to get rid of the hated space station. Everyone seemed to have their own reasons for hating the ring around the Earth. For some it was the environmental angle, for others it was the social-economic injustice of the system, and for some of the others, they were just pissed off about life.

Tonight the meeting centered around a resolution circulating among the different chapters that called for, once again, the dismantling of the Equatorial Station. It was the third time in the last five years the resolution had been put forward. Twice it had been agreed upon and sent to the I.C.N. - and ignored. Very few people believed this latest effort would succeed any better.

Terry was taking advantage of this moment

to rally the Joshua Tree chapter to support an alternative, unofficial resolution. The unofficial resolution called for all-out revolution, for destroying the gravity lifts and crashing the E.S. Was it do-able? Not likely, but that wasn't the point. The alternative resolution had been put forward by the I.S.I. as a way to entrap people into violating the recently enacted Anti-Treason Acts for Global Security. This was just a clean-up operation to remove the BDTRC and its members as a potential threat.

Much to Terry's disappointment, and against his threats of resigning from the group, the Joshua Tree chapter voted for the resolution to use legitimate means and against the alternative resolution. Terry was so pissed off he went home that evening cursing to himself about "worthless revolutionaries". He wrote up false reports against all the various members, and had arrest warrants issued for them the next day.

Jeremy weaved his way back to his apartment. On most nights the hallways were usually deserted after 7:00 p.m., except for dog walkers. Yet another law no one paid attention to anymore: Civil Code 7248.6 – No Dogs Permitted on Equatorial Station. *It's probably dog hair creating all these dust balls*, Jeremy thought, as if this was some unforgivable transgression. The long day of drinking hadn't improved his mood one bit.

Jeremy continued to bumble his way down the hallway, as he approached his apartment it sensed his presence, opened the door, prepared a fresh drink for him, and turned on the TV. Jeremy landed on the sofa with a fresh drink already sitting on the side table waiting for him, and the TV playing the local news.

Jeremy checked his e-mail to see if anyone had responded to his property questions. He brought up the classified ads on the TV and scanned again for houses in the desert, like he did most nights. He was hoping to get that intuitive feeling telling him that he had found what he was looking for. Of course, he had this feeling many times before, only to realize later it was a false alarm. Just a bubble of hope and nothing more. Still, he watched videos of different properties nearly every night, waiting for the one.

The next morning his wake-up alarm went off, but Jeremy was deeply asleep. A property video played over and over again on the TV, the last one in his search the night before. His drink sat untouched on the side table. Jeremy was slumped over the sofa, still in his suit. It would be several more hours before Jeremy woke up – hung over from his long day of drinking – unaware that his life had taken an unexpected downward turn.

Evan Blake looked over the morning report, he wasn't happy. Jeremy Alexander was absent again. Third time this month, if he remembered correctly. And this was just one of the many symptoms of decline listed in the report. Evan hated seeing a long-term management team member faltering. He had seen it repeatedly in his twenty-seven years on the E.S. working for the Station Services Corporation.

For many managers the symptoms showed up around the sixth year – the missed days of work, the vague maintenance reports, the rumors of kickbacks and bribes, and the drinking. Why did this job drive so many good people to drink? Evan hadn't figured that one out yet.

The morning report had a several-page supplementary report on Jeremy: his general habits, a list of his TV searches, and the various videos he had watched over the last week. Evan had seen these patterns before. The fact that he had really thought Jeremy was potentially upper-management material made him sad. *What a waste,* he thought as he signed the report, checking the box next to the words, "dispose of immediately – export to the surface." Better to take care of this problem now rather than later. The corporation expected 100% commitment, nothing less would do.

That checked-off box set off a series of events, none of them good for Jeremy. Suddenly, without his awareness, he entered the labyrinth of the employee disposal system of the Station Services Corporation. A transfer warrant was issued for him and an employee disposal team was sent to his known residence. While he slept soundly on his sofa, arrangements were already being made to move him to a transfer detainment facility on the planet below, near Barstow in the state of California, a Pacific coastal region of the North American Alliance. Paperwork was written up, orders sent, and teams of defense lawyers deployed according to the standard human rights procedures that governed these types of employee disposals. Everything had to be legal, not necessarily fair, but it had to be legal.

Jeremy woke up to the sight of a dozen members of the disposal team pointing their rifles at him. These proceedings weren't intended

to be polite. "Subdue and detain the target" was Rule No.1 and "Shoot to kill" was Rule No.2. Evan hated it when they had to resort to Rule No.2, but you had to do what you had to do – he hoped he didn't have to this time.

Jeremy lifted his arms above his head. He had no idea what was going on, but having a dozen or so rifles pointed at his head was not a good thing. His head was ringing like a bell and his tongue felt big and dry in his mouth. The light coming in the windows was hurting his eyes – he sneezed several times from the glare as he looked at the silhouettes of the disposal team around him with their guns. None of this made sense, so he surrendered – waiting – with his arms in the air, waiting for the inevitable handcuffs and whatever came next.

Through the glare of light Jeremy saw the figure of his boss, Mr. Blake, surrounded by the I.S.I. officers holding their rifles. "Good afternoon, Mr. Alexander," said Evan, hating what he had to do next. One of the disposal team members put handcuffs on Jeremy and hauled him to his feet. *Okay, this is work related...* Jeremy thought, confused because this seemed a little over-the-top for skipping out on an afternoon of work to have a drink or two.

"Mr. Alexander, a range of information has been brought to the corporation's attention about your recent behavioral patterns. Behavioral patterns which we have seen over and over during the lifetime of the E.S." Evan paused for a moment to make sure Jeremy was paying attention, "Due to standard procedures, orders have been issued for your disposal. Your position with the corporation has been terminated, you are to be exported to the planet below, immediately."

Jeremy had heard of this procedure before, but it never happened to anyone he knew personally. Every so often an employee would disappear, then a team of movers packed up the employee's apartment and removed its contents

to somewhere – who knows where? But this kind
of thing only happened to dissidents, malcon-
tents, those with a revolutionary, anti-authority
bent – those that couldn't hack it in management.
It didn't happen to people like Jeremy, whatever
that meant, but it was a thought swimming
through his confused, hungover and sleepy mind.
The handcuffs locked on his wrists with a resol-
ute click and someone injected something, a drug
of some kind, into his arm causing him to fall
back into a deep sleep.

That was the last thing Jeremy experienced
on the Equatorial Station. While he slept from
the effects of the injection, his body was trans-
ported down a gravity lift to the surface, flown to
a transfer station in Barstow, and processed according to the disposal plan.

Jeremy had a number of disturbing dreams –
profound in nature – while under the effects of
the drugs during the transport process. From the
moment he woke up several days later on the
surface – in a transfer dorm in California – every
fiber of his being was committed to destroying
the E.S. and the system it represented.

Due to a clerical error, Jeremy's transfer papers ended up being routed into the I.C.N. Crim-
inal Justice System. From there, a number of
unfortunate mistakes were made that caused

Jeremy to be transferred to the nearby prison on a faulty treason conviction. It would be many confusing months before he started to recover from the shock of the rapid, and unjust, turn of events. By then he was on his way to a new kind of life – with a distinct mission.

It was seven years later when Jeremy exited the prison facility in Barstow, California. Much had changed. His hair and beard were long and hung down over his plain robes. His name was now Baba Sri Ravi, and he had a growing cult-like following. He had become a well-known, self-styled revolutionary guru.

Nearly 300 people were waiting for him to exit the prison gates on this bright spring morning of 2092. They all waited in the bright sunlight to see their guru, the revolutionary mystic, the accidental leader, the divine dreamer – among other names.

Baba Sri Ravi looked out over the group of people gathered to meet him and smiled, beatifically, with the knowing look of a holy man. His plan might work out after all.

Three, two, one... he counted to himself, and then he felt the tear of a bullet cut through his gut, and then another through his left leg.

Yes, he thought as he collapsed to the ground with blood pouring out of the wounds, forming into pools. *Yes, this is working out perfectly...* Another bullet cut through his heart and Baba Sri Ravi smiled, beatifically.

After all, he knew it was coming. Everyone knew it was coming. Baba Sri Ravi had prophesied it himself five years earlier, during the early years of his mistaken incarceration, around the time he had changed his name. He had seen it in a dream, like many of his prophecies and visions. Over and over he had sent out messages telling the growing number of followers that after he died he would come back to life and bring down the E.S. It was pretty far-fetched, but to hear Baba Sri Ravi tell it in the messages that got out from prison, you could almost see it yourself in your head.

Several people had come out of prison during the last few years, people who had spent time with Baba Sri Ravi, and they were firm believers in his mystical power. They said there was something different about this man; he had gone through some kind of transformation they couldn't understand or explain. For one, they had seen him walk through walls – out of the prison, and then he had come back. He was staying in prison, not because he had to, but because he had his own reasons. That alone was enough for anyone of them to become a believer in the powers of Baba Sri Ravi.

For seven years, Jeremy/Baba had meditated and prepared himself. He had seen the vision over and over again. Sometimes it would tell the story one way, sometimes it would be told with other metaphors. The details changed but the story was basically always the same – death, rebirth, destruction and renewal – like some eternal loop. The gun shots, the taste of death, the in-between passage, the return as a super-empowered being, and the crashing end of the Equatorial Station, the renewal of society. Always the same series of events.

The I.S.I. was also aware of Baba Sri Ravi's messages from prison. They immediately took possession of his body and had it cremated within a few hours. Not that they were really expecting him to come back as a super-empowered being, but they weren't taking any chances. His ashes were hoisted to the top of a gravity elevator and shot off into deep space, in multiple packages, in multiple directions. Just to be safe. Meanwhile, a slow panic spread through the E.S., and within days people started to evacuate the station in noticeable numbers.

———————●———————

Baba Sri Ravi wandered through the maintenance corridors of the E.S. Every so often he would materialize at a computer station, type a few things into the computer as he hummed a little song to himself, then dematerialize, and wander on. He took his time. He really didn't have to hurry now. People were leaving the station and that was a good thing. He didn't hate people quite as much as he used to – the changes over the last seven years had mellowed him.

Over the next several months, as many of the people on the E.S. evacuated to the surface, Baba Sri Ravi wandered the whole of the station, stopping at maintenance computers around the ring to enter instructions and special codes. No one saw him at work, nor did anyone expect such a situation. Before long he had complete control of the maintenance and stabilization of the entire station. The controls lay dormant – concealed inside the operating system – just waiting for his coded message to bring the whole machine down through a collapse in the network of gravity lift stations and their maintenance of the stability of the Equatorial Station's position. Once the message was sent to the system the collapse would begin, piece by piece, until the entire station was torn apart and thrown out into space. Some, a small portion, of the station would fall back to the surface, but most of it would be carried away from the planet by the release of the gravity lifts in a carefully planned order.

At least that was the plan, until Baba Sri Ravi felt himself begin to disintegrate. His essence was slowly dissolving and losing its ability to maintain a presence in this world. This was completely unexpected.

Before he realized what was going on, he was whisked down the long tunnel of the afterlife, processed for a new incarnation, and on his way back to Earth as a newborn infant named Jerry Allen. He didn't remember his previous incarnation, at least not until the time he entered kindergarten.

———●———

Jerry started his job in the maintenance crew of the E.S. soon after his eighteenth birthday, and just weeks before the station's seventy-fifth anniversary. He was part of the programming crew responsible for upgrading the old computer system. No one knew that Baba Sri Ravi had returned to finish his prophecy.

When the end came it was spectacular. Various reports stated afterwards that the computer system had been compromised during the up-grade, which led to the loss in stability. Though it was a near universal agreement that the computer had been majorly responsible for the destruction of the station, experts had noted that the pattern of collapse had been, coincidentally, in such a way as to eliminate ninety percent of the possible Earth-related devastation, sending most of the debris out into space. The odds of that happening were more than a million to one. No one paid much attention to the statistic.

Fucking
Like Animals

Jean-Paul L. Garnier

❝ You'll have to wait in the hallway for a few minutes, I've got some business to finish up in here with an associate. Better yet, go get us a cup of coffee and come back in twenty minutes, I should be ready for you then." said Derek dismissively, closing the door on Danny's face.

Danny had no choice but to walk down the street for the coffee. You couldn't argue with someone who was in Derek's line of work. Dealers always had to be in control, always acting like their business was more important than it is. Danny didn't mind, the clubs wouldn't be opening for hours, he was planning ahead, really wanting the night to go his way, and knowing that the pills took a few hours to kick in. He grabbed two cups of old coffee at the donut store, poured copious amounts of sugar into them, and started back for Derek's apartment.

"OK come on in, Danny." Derek barked through the intercom.

Multiple deadbolts rattled before Danny was let in to the dark apartment. One of those places where you can't tell what time it is because the room has never seen the light of day, at least not with its current occupant. He strolled in and sat on the couch, taking the bong that Derek handed him and inhaling a huge hit from the water pipe.

Smoke trailed from Danny's mouth as his eyes grew visibly redder and his voice deepened half an octave. They both lit cigarettes and sat smoking in silence, pretending to be friends, but really having nothing to say. When the obligatory courtesies were over Danny nervously breached the subject.

"Do you have any more of that *Bird* stuff? You weren't kidding about that shit, it really got me going." Danny asked enthusiastically, his tone back to normal.

"What did I tell you? I always have the best and newest stuff. I don't have the same shit as last time, but I've got a different strain of *Bird* that I know you'll dig." said Derek dismissing Danny's comment and rifling through a wooden box that he kept under his recliner chair.

Danny watched as smoke curled to the ceiling, knowing that Derek did not like to be interrupted while exploring his stash, "Last time I saw you I went to Club Intra, and man, that shit really worked like you said it would. I was out there cutting-a-rug like never before, and just like you said, the girls sure did notice. I had a fucking circle of people around me watching me dance, can you believe it? The Friday before last, no one even noticed I was alive and out there on the dance floor."

"Of course you were, like I said I have the

best *Bird* in town. Here's the new strain, made from some jungle variety. You know, it's the ones you've never heard of that have the craziest effects. Probably seen it on the nature channel or something, they use it the same way we do, works for them too." said Derek while waving the small baggy in Danny's direction.

Danny grabbed the bag, putting on his least threatening air, trying not to agitate the high-strung dealer, "Is this one going to have the same effects? I mean, I really liked that last stuff, and I'm hoping for a similar experience. Sure you don't have any more of that last shit?"

"Ran out shortly after I saw you last. Don't worry, you're gonna flip when you try this. From what I understand this variety will have you dancing even harder, and they'll notice, I guarantee it." Derek held out his hand as he spoke. His way of saying that a conversation was over and it was time to pay up and leave. There were probably a few people waiting out in the hallway as Danny had before.

He handed over the money and took the baggie, slapped Derek a high-five and hit the street, still with several hours to go before he could show up fashionably late at Club Intra.

———●———

"You feel like going out with me tonight, Darling? I'm going to the club to meet up with some of the girls, you're welcome to join us if you like." asked Clara.

"I wish I could, but you already know that I'm on graveyard shift again tonight. While you'll be having drinks, I'll be packing boxes. You have fun, Cutie. We'll just have to catch up in the morning. I have to leave after this cup of coffee, do you want a glass of wine before you're off too?" replied Frank.

"Yes please." shouted Clara from the bathroom as she flat-ironed her hair and primed for her night out. Secretly she was glad that Frank had to work. He wasn't as much fun as he used to be before he had taken his new job. He was always tired now, and rarely felt like dancing, always complaining that her night was his morning, and who would want to dance first thing in the morning.

He set the glass of wine on the bathroom counter and ran his fingers through her still warm hair, gave her a peck on the cheek so as not to smear her newly applied lipstick, and patted her on the ass, then left for work worrying that he would be late.

A wave of relief flooded over Clara as she heard his car speed up the driveway and out into the street. She would have the whole night without him and planned to cut loose. She'd been tied up in the house too long, and if he wasn't going to go out to the clubs it wouldn't stop her from having a good time. She took a Xanax from her purse and washed it down with the wine, draining the glass with one swig, then slid to the kitchen for a refill. She was going to start this night relaxed and feeling good.

The line to get into Club Intra went all the way around the block. Seas of dolled up girls and drooling guys smoked endless waves of cigarettes as they waited and prayed to get in. Clara met with her friends Janet and Sarah in the parking lot and passed a bottle around in the car, getting their buzz on, and saving money at the bar. Not that any of them would have to pay for their drinks once they got inside. After drinking for half an hour and killing a pint of vodka they made their way to the line.

"Hey! You, three ladies over there. You can come to the front of the line." shouted the bouncer. It wasn't the first time that the girls had been flagged from the line and allowed to get in without waiting. One of the perks of being sexy females.

———————●———————

The girls' luck wasn't as good with the line at the bar. They fell into their place and waited while people-watching and chatting it up. Several times Janet pointed out guys in the crowd that caught her eye, she was always on the prowl. When one particularly hot guy walked by she couldn't contain herself any longer, "A girl ought to be able to get lucky at a place like this, Intra is always crawling with fresh blood." The girls all laughed and hooted at the guy that had walked by, their voices fading into the loud music and crowd noise.

When they were half way through the line Sarah pulled out a small baggie containing three pink pills with brown flecks, "You guys want to try some *Cat*, it's the latest thing on the street, just picked it up from a friend, says not too many people have even heard of it yet. It's supposed to get you going real good, like *Molly* but better."

Without further conversation the girls divvied up the pills, not waiting for their drinks to wash them down, swallowing them dry. Just then they caught the bartender's eye and the vodka continued to flow. They staked out a table on the edge of the dance floor, sitting with their drinks and waiting for the *Cat* to kick in, while eyeing

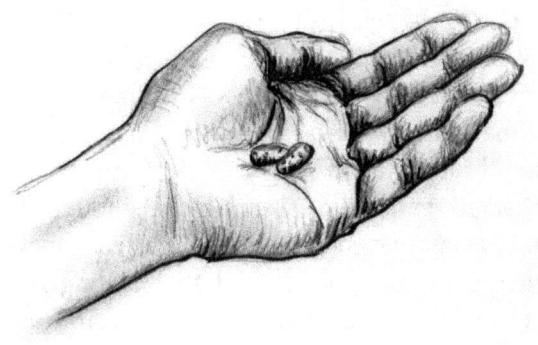

prospective men and making fun of those with less than graceful dance moves.

The drinks were already working, and the new sensation of *Cat* also began to pulse through their bodies, perking their minds. The feeling was sharp and came on like needles all over the body, or like the sick thrill of a leg filled with sleep coming back to life.

"I feel sleek." Clara was the first to announce the head change.

"Predatory." followed Janet.

"I told you that you guys would love this shit. Wait until it kicks in full force, we're gonna be slinking around that dance floor like we never have before." said Sarah proudly. She always took pride in having the latest thing in her pocket, always hungry for new experience and someone to share it with.

When Clara got up to go to the bathroom she realized that her movement was different. Each step that she took was more like a leap. She glided through the crowd with an accuracy that she had never known, sliding right through the gaps between dancers, never rubbing shoulders. As her body curved she had the fleeting epiphany that she must look good from across the room. She was slicker than ever. Sexy.

Arriving back at the table she could see by the look on her friend's face that the drug was kicking in for her too. Janet had already made her way to the floor and was rubbing up against the hottie that had passed them at the bar. In the flashing lights Clara could tell that he was not as cute as they had thought in the dim light, but Janet didn't seem to mind and was getting pretty fresh in a hurry.

"You wanna go dance too, looks like fun?" asked Sarah.

Clara was eager, but not quite ready, "Let's have one more drink and then join her, I feel like getting fucked up tonight."

The waiter plopped two more vodka tonics

in front of them and asked about their tab before leaving them alone again. The girls sipped on the drinks and chatted about love-life problems for a minute before deciding to switch the topic of conversation to something more light-hearted and fun. As Sarah was telling her about a new Joe she had met, Clara noticed a guy out on the dance floor, not far off from where Janet was still dancing.

The man was dancing with wild abandon, moving like nothing she had ever seen. He looked so loose, like he was really enjoying himself no matter what was going on around him. Clara wanted to be that free too, she couldn't remember the last time she had had a good time the way that the dancing fellow was. His moves were so alluring, like they were designed to draw one in, they had a hypnotic suggestion to them and they were working their magic on her. She had the sudden and irresistible need to pounce on the dancer, to encompass him. Now she understood the "predatory" comment that Janet had made, it was coming on strong.

She looked to Sarah and announced, "See that dancing fool over there, he's got a thing. I'm gonna go dance with him, would you mind checking in my coat with yours?" Without waiting for a reply she downed the last of her vodka tonic and made her way across the dance floor to the guy that had caught her attention.

He moved wildly, arms and legs flowing in such a way that it hardly looked human, but still with an appealing and odd grace to the movements. He knew the moonwalk, not to mention a score of other moves that were not in the book. He seemed tireless and energetic, even the sweat on his brow had some kind of natural allure. Clara's back arched as she approached him, she decided not to say anything but just to join in the dance.

She almost had a difficult time keeping up with him, but the *Cat* pulsing through her kept her vibrant and alert. She mirrored some of his moves, surprised that she had such abilities at dance. When she fell short he guided her, twirling her with such speed that it made her giddy and elated. They danced through endless songs, she forgetting all about the friends she had come with, and he focusing all of his attention on her. Clara didn't care what music was playing. She was centered on him, without even knowing his name. He was like prey in crosshairs of her mind. Images of pouncing him flooded her thoughts.

Drenched with sweat he asked her if she would like to grab another drink at the bar.

"Why don't we leave instead?" she sugges-
ted, the images still running through her.

His smile said an eager yes as he shouted
over the music, "By the way, my name is Danny,
what's yours?"

Clara forgot all about the coat check as they
headed for the door.

———————●———————

Clara rode Danny with the ferocity of a wo-
men pent up, climbing on top of him, every
nerve of her body trying to rock his world in a
way he had never known.

"Hey slow down a little bit, I want to enjoy
it." breathed Danny heavily.

Danny displayed none of the prowess that he
had on the dance floor. Still she didn't slow
down and he came in three anti-climactic spurts,
the whole event being over in several fleeting
moments. He rolled over and passed out whispering something about *Bird* that she couldn't
have understood even if she had been paying attention.

*Fuck. That was hardly worth it. Didn't even
get to toy with him. I can't believe I just cheated
on Frank for that lousy lay. He didn't even seem
to like me that much, just fell right asleep. At*

least this was the only time. I mean, last time didn't count cuz it was only drunken kissing. And the other thing… This time I really took it there, it must be the drugs. That's it, it was the drugs.

"Cutie, I'm home. I've got a treat for you." announced Frank on his way into the apartment. His cry was met by silence. The house was empty.

She must have gotten drunk and stayed with one of the girls. I hope they weren't drunk driving all night. She must be safe. I'll let her sleep it off then give her a call.

Frank got ready for bed as the rest of the world was waking, had his morning glass of wine then went to sleep trying to drown out the hustle and bustle of the now awake city with pleasant thoughts.

When he awoke the bed was still empty. Disturbed, he crawled into the shower to get ready for another long night of toiling away with shipping and receiving. He dressed himself and was about to run out the door when Clara arrived, make-up smeared face, and reeking like alcohol.

"Fun night huh, Cutie? Looks like you really

got into it. Where'd you stay last night, I was starting to get worried about you. And where's the coat that I gave you, you were wearing it last night?" questioned Frank.

"I stayed out at Janet's place. They were way too drunk to drive me home, I think I left my jacket in Sarah's car. We had a great time at Intra. So many new people showing up there all of the time. You should really come with us sometime." said Clara casually.

"Yeah, if I ever get a night off! I gotta run off to work now. You look like you could use a little rest, I'll see you in the morning, OK." Grabbing his bag he headed out the door to his old beater.

———⬤———

"Look, Derek, this stuff worked great on the dance floor, but it made me a two-pump-chump. What the hell?" said Danny.

"Maybe you just aren't getting enough." replied Derek with his particular brand of condescension.

"The *Bird* you gave me last time was a scam, what good is getting the girls if you can't enjoy them afterwards?"

"OK, Danny, I've got what you need. You just let Doctor Derek fix you up. You know I've got a solution for everything. Wait until you hear what I've got up my sleeve."

"If it's more of that last *Bird* you had I don't want it, that shit caused me problems. I'll bet it's the last time I score with this chick I met, and she was smoking!" interrupted Danny.

"Just let me finish, Son. You still want the *Bird*, I guarantee it. But this time you gotta try *Rat* with it. Ever hear of those rodents, or marsupials, or whatever they are, that fuck for weeks straight? Well you're gonna screw like one of them if you take this stuff. You can take it with the *Bird*, use your dancing to lure 'em in, then finish the job with this stuff," Derek beamed with showy confidence as he took out two small baggies for Danny to try. "The *Rat* is on me, let me know how it works out, I've had nothing but good reports."

Danny took the bags and handed over his money. Derek didn't usually mess around, so he figured that what he said would go. He'd find out this Friday at any rate.

——●——

Clara hung up the phone after a brief conversation with Sarah that ended with promises of more *Cat*.

"We're going to Intra again, Darling, you gotta work?"

"Yep, you know that. You guys are going there again, don't you ever get enough of that place?" replied Frank.

"I like the music they play there, and the drinks are reasonable. I'll probably be here until after you leave, Janet is picking me up and you know how she is always way late. Would you like me to make you some breakfast before you head out to work?" The last bit with a tinge of resentment, she was sick of catering to him. She rarely even got to see him and he was always so tired that he stayed in a perpetual condition of acting short with her.

"No thanks, Cutie, I'll pick up something on the way to work. You have fun with the girls, try not to stay out so late this time so I can actually hang out with you between shifts." And he was gone again, leaving her in the empty apartment with nothing to do but wait and get into the wine early.

———●———

"Hey, Clara, isn't that the guy you went home with last time we were here?" asked Janet.

Clara hesitated before stuttering, "Uh, yeah, I think so, it's kinda blurry to me."

"Well that guy sure can dance, look at him out there, I'll bet he was good in bed too…" joined Sarah.

"Not really, anyway shut up about it, and keep quiet around Frank. The real highlight of last week was the *Cat*. I've been dying to get into some more, you'll have to introduce me to the guy you get it from," Clara grinned impatiently, "I'll go get us some drinks." She stood up and headed for the bar, eager for the sleek of *Cat*.

"Can I get those drinks for you, Baby?" A bold stranger stood next to her at the bar, money in hand, leg beating to the music.

"Thanks, Buddy!" called out Clara as she gripped the three glasses in her hands and walked away from the stranger before he could ask another question. She was getting good at this, and the *Cat* wasn't even inside of her yet. The evening was going to flow.

She set down the drinks in front of the girls and Sarah handed her a pill. "Bottoms up." Three glasses slammed down on the table simultaneously, the night was about to begin. Clara opened her purse and pulled out a compact to check her face. The inside of her purse was illuminated by the blue light of her cell. She pulled out the phone and checked the texts.

<Have fun, Angel. Hopefully I'll be off work

by six thirty, if I'm lucky they might even let me go early. Kiss>

What timing. It's like he knows and wants me to feel guilty for having a good time. Just because he's a stick in the mud doesn't mean that I can't party and have a good time. He's so boring he probably wouldn't even give Cat a try. He belongs at work.

Clara put aside these thoughts and went back to focusing on having a good time. As usual Janet was already on the dance floor, not even waiting for the *Cat* to kick in.

Sarah spoke first, "How are you and Frank doing? I mean, Brian and I aren't getting on so well. I just can't understand it, he's always eaten with jealousy. It's like he wished he could be as cool as me or something…"

Clara nodded and said yeah at all the appropriate times, but heard none of it. The sleekness had returned and her eyes fixed on Danny across the room. He was spinning like a top, alive and on fire. A group of girls danced, cooing next to him. Brow wet with perspiration he glistened like fresh bait waiting to be hooked. She felt a sudden surge of predatory rage at the sight of the other girls. No one was going to beat her out on this one.

She slid across the floor and cut between the

girls and Danny. He didn't notice her right away, lost in the trance of dancing. He opened his eyes as Clara brushed up against him, making sure to put a bit of hip into it. She had his attention now.

She seems so much bigger than before, as if I'm looking at her from below. It must be the drugs. This cocktail has me flying. Derek wasn't kidding about the mix, I feel even better than before. Last time she didn't seem that into me. But she's back for more. The dancing is working, the Rat better work too!

A circle cleared around them as they danced. They moved like animals, dripping and ferocious. Others were clearly amused and envious of the grace they were displaying, dancing as if they were years away from being strangers. The music beat them into a frenzy, arms, legs, and hips moving with such speed that the music almost seemed too slow to keep up with them. Clara lifted a leg and wrapped it around Danny's waist pulling him closer. She needed to devour him, not sure if she could even wait until they were out of the club.

This Cat is stronger than the last batch. I still can't believe that I can move this way. And he is such a good dancer, last time was no fluke. Frank would probably be cowering in the corner wanting to leave by now. It's good he's not here, I have a hunger that is gonna need a large bite-of-life to satiate. I feel so free.

Clara briefly caught sight of her friends, now both sitting at the table. Both had looks of amazement and envy on their faces sweaty from dancing. They egged her on with a few lewd gestures, gave the signal that meant 'do you want another drink' and at the shake of her head went back to scanning the room for guys of their own. She didn't need any more liquor for now, she was drunk on life, and *Cat*. And she had found her mouse.

Danny's legs were like jelly. Glancing at his watch he realized that he had been on the dance floor without a break for hours. He still felt fresh, but sweat was pouring down his chest, the same chest that concealed his rapid heartbeat. An irresistible desire to make savage love to Clara took over his senses, but she didn't look finished dancing.

I wonder how much longer I can hold out and still have stamina for her. She was a wild one last week, and she's still got that barbaric look in her eye. The Bird and Rat should keep me going if Derek really knows what he's talking about. Maybe I should offer her a drink and cool down for a second. But we are in flames, and everyone around us can tell.

"I'll be right back." Clara whispered in his ear. She made off towards the table where Sarah and Janet sat talking.

"Looks like you got yourself a catch again." said Janet with a touch of jealousy.

Clara ignored the comment and looked to Sarah, "Do you have any more *Cat*, I really want to take it there, tonight's my night."

Sarah looked slightly disappointed, "Yeah I've got one left, I was planning on taking tomorrow. I guess if you can pay me back for it right now I'd be willing to part with it."

Without hesitation Clara pulled out her wallet and made the exchange. Moving slower than she had on the dance floor made her realize how sweaty wet she was, and she headed towards the bathroom to rinse off and wash down another dose of *Cat*.

She emerged from the bathroom after several minutes and spread her gaze around the floor looking for Danny. Her eyes fixed on several cute guys as she scanned the crowd, possibly other prospects for later. From every angle men stared at her, desire beaming and indiscriminate. She had that air about her tonight. Something about the *Cat* stirred something inside of you, and men had no problem noticing.

Where is that guy? He better not have left

while I was in the bathroom. I wonder if I was in there longer than I thought. I guess I could find another victim.

As Clara considered her options Danny emerged from the crowd to her left. The place was packed and it was no wonder that she hadn't noticed him. But her mind was fixed on one thing and one thing only, herself. When she saw him her senses lit up and the predatory feeling rose again into her belly with incomprehensible force. She forgot all about the other guys in the club and slinked towards him, sliding between bodies as if they weren't there at all, as if only the two of them existed, in separate worlds, but with the intimate relationship that only prey and predator can share.

There she is, I'd thought I'd lost her. His heart thumped against his chest in quick short bursts. *I hope she wants to leave, I feel like I can't wait. She seems bigger than before and she's so hot. If it's anything like before I shouldn't have any problem scoring.*

Their bodies came together again, bare skin slipping, clothes clinging to their moisture. The circle opened for them. Bass rumbled through the floor, rhythm moved their legs. Their arms found their way to each other. Dancing was beginning to not be enough.

———●———

"Do you want a drink?" slurred Danny.

"Got any vodka?" the slurring continued.

"Yeah, what do you want for mixer?"

"Straight's fine."

Clara went to the bathroom to splash water on her face as the drinks were being poured. *It's damn hot in here. It's gonna make me sick.* Staggering to the toilet there was no time to raise the seat. Vomit sprayed the lid and the surrounding wall. Splashing water on her face she gathered herself enough to find a washcloth and clean the muck. *Damn it Clara, this is your moment, get it together.* Without rinsing her mouth she strode towards the living room where Danny waited with the drinks. She half fell towards the couch and into his lap as French disco pop teased her ringing ears.

She watched Danny's mouth move while he spoke, but didn't take in a word. She didn't care what he had to say, she wanted only one thing. Sip after sip of the vodka cooled her back down and made her body settle into the couch where she lay. *Why hurry, I've got all night. I might as well make this guy swell and make him wait.* She didn't owe this guy anything, but she was going to have her fun. Leaning over to kiss him she spilled a bit of her drink on his lap. "So sorry." she half mused while running her hand over the wet spot in his crotch. He rose under her touch as she noticed that the skin on his face glistened and flushed bronze.

Clara bit at his ear while whispering for another drink. *She's toying with me, but I can wait. She's definitely going to put out.* Danny stood up and walked awkwardly to the kitchen. His gait betraying his arousal. "Mind if I put on another record?" Clara asked half-heartedly as she pushed play on the CD she had already selected. Notes poured out of the speakers and into her throbbing senses. *Frank would hate this music.* But she was loving it, letting it flow through her, almost forgetting about Danny all together. Until he returned with the drink. Throwing back her head she gulped at the vodka, drinking with an air of authority, wanting to look like a pro in the overly eager man's eyes. He seemed nervous and leaning her head on his chest she could feel the rapid beating of his heart.

I've got this guy in the palm of my hand.

While she wasn't looking Danny slipped another *Rat* into his mouth and swallowed hard. *I'm not risking blowing this.* Clara didn't notice or she might have asked to try one too. Instead she loosened his belt and slid it off of his pants.

He lifted himself slightly from the couch, allowing her to do so. When the belt hung limp in her hand she slapped his thigh with it. "Ahhhh!" surprise got the best of him. Before he could speak she clawed at his neck, pulling him into her and joining their lips. He rose again and reached for her breast.

With speed and accuracy she didn't know she had she slapped his hand away.

"Easy girl…" Danny slurred.

Clara put her hand to his lips and stopped his words with a finger in his mouth. With her other hand she teased him through his pants. She straddled him and bit at his neck before pulling him onto the floor. He fell on top of her and moved in for a kiss. This she avoided and rolled to position herself on top of him once more. Buttons popped and flew in every direction as she tore his shirt out of her way. His chest also shown bronze. Clara ran her tongue across it, tasting the salt of his perspiration.

It was obvious that Danny wanted to switch positions and bend Clara over the couch, but she didn't give him the opportunity. She pulled his pants down just enough to reveal his equipment. Not wanting to waste time on undressing she hiked her skirt and pulled her panties aside, forgetting all about the rubbers in her purse. And she rode.

She moved like she was alone. Screwing so openly that she might have well been by herself masturbating. He had more in him this time and she was going to take advantage. Then she noticed him. *Uh, his face looks bloated. And so sweaty. Is that normal?*

Danny felt tremors in his arms, legs and back and mistook them for a precursor to orgasm. *Hold on champ, you're doing better than last time.* His heart pounded, he thought he might faint. So awake but drowsy at the same time. For a moment he forgot what was going on. Then his confusion focused into an acute headache. *Get it together, man. Got to enjoy this while you can.* Danny was wishing he had avoided that last drink. Incredible thirst overtook him. The room seemed too hot. *Just hold on a minute. Almost there.*

Blue light seared behind Danny eyes as he ejaculated in one final thrust and fell limp. Clara felt the hot outpour flood inside of her. *Did he just cum in me? Crap!* She leapt up from his crotch. "What are you thinking?" she demanded.

He responded with silence. Already losing the heat that his body had been exuding. She repeated herself, and again silence. Purple streaks rose from his skin all over his body and his face seemed even more swollen than before. *This isn't good*. She struggled for her purse and grabbed her phone. Another text.

<You OK, Baby? It's late and I haven't heard from you yet.>

What timing. She ignored the text and dialed.

"911 emergency."

In between deep gasps she managed to say, "I need an ambulance right away. A heart attack, or an OD or something."

The next minutes disappeared into a flood of despairing thought. When she finally looked up an EMT was repeating his question to her, "What have you guys been taking tonight?"

His tone induced her into a new state of semi-clarity. "I don't know about him, but I was taking *Cat*. And we were both drinking heavily." Lying wasn't going to do any good here.

"You kids and these animal hormones, who in the world would think that taking that stuff was a good idea. Jim, we've got another endocrine failure on our hands. I think we lost him already, try a shot of adrenaline. And we should be taking you in too, that stuff is dangerous."

"If I have a choice I'll just be on my way. I don't even know this guy." Clara texted for a cab while speaking.

———————•———————

Clara hung up the phone with the doctor and immediately called Sarah, "You remember a few months ago when I left with that guy? How I told you he came in me when he died?"

"Yeah, you poor thing. It's so horrible I can't believe it." Sarah had already heard the story a few times and knew that Clara was having a hard time digesting all of it.

"I just got off the phone with the clinic. It's so much worse than I thought. I missed my period, so I went in for a pregnancy test and…"

Sarah interrupted, "Oh no! You're pregnant? What are you going to do?"

"It's worse than that. The doctor said that it's some kind of fluke. He said I make Octomom look normal. I'm pregnant with ten babies. He called it a litter. And said that my body couldn't possibly handle the stress. I'm going to have to abort." Her voice was choking up and the words came between increasing sobs.

"Oh my God, Girl. It's terrible. Don't worry I'll be there for you. Whatever you do just don't tell Frank. You don't need him making this mess worse. Do you want me to come over?" Her question was returned with sobbing.

Sarah hung up the phone and dialed Janet to spread the news.

The Banshee

Jakes Bayley

2/19 4:32 PM

Aisha,

Greetings from the edge of the world. Frightfully boring. I'm lodged in a little 18th century cottage just outside town with no signal and piss-poor wifi. St. David's Town is predictable— tourists and 'pilgrims' seem more interested in plastic tokens of british 'culture' and kebabs than supposed gods or ghosts... found what looks to be a pretty ace chippy though. How's Majorca? Zivi's been driving me fucking mad demanding progress even tho I told him monday. Please let me know what you think of attachment. Pls chk for tone... IE appropriately cuntish:)

x -Iv

(Attached file)

The Welsh coast can be a rugged reminder of a lost Britain: a mossy, mist-cloaked stone land of monks, dragons, and marauding Vikings. Every year, tourists flock here to graze on this land of memory (expand blah blah)— but this year they've been joined by an entirely different procession.

Ever since three Polish girls on a church-

sponsored field trip claimed to have been guided by the sound of unseen bells to the sight of a cloaked woman mysteriously hovering above the waves near Bosherton, the usually quiet seaside region has experienced a rash of questionable reports: bizarre tricks of the sun, sudden darkness, strange sounds echoing from the cliffsides, and— of course— more floating ladies.

notes: mass hysteria, group hallucination, etc.: brief history (bloody argot in the fish batter?!) - sundogs/parhelia, solar flares?,etc. (will expand)

2/19 7:44 PM

Aisha,

Ha! Just got back from that ace chippy. more like arse. I've found the soggiest fish ever to roam the earth. Place had a typically welsh (i.e. unpronounceable) name, 'drywd' or summat... staffed by pasty brexiteers who could smell the Remainer in me. The atmosphere is rotten. Sometimes feel that London may be the last refuge of sanity on earth (imagine that, I know). Walked the beach for an hour. Mist seems to have driven away the pilgrims for now. At this point I think the girls were simply lying (they certainly are getting plenty of attention, see BBC

1 tonight) although I did see a bit of blue plastic tarp hanging from a floating marker off the coast. Wouldn't that be rich. Off to find a fucking curry. pls see attached, and thanks for the input- I'll try being a little more cuntish;)

x

-Iv

PS just read the girls have been whisked off to the Vatican? Smells like they'll be getting their story straight. I'm going to spend the night at the rocks tonight (if I get bored and head back to the cottage early, don't you tell a soul:)

2/20 8:17 AM

Aisha,

Well last night was exhausting in every way. It was so cold my fingers don't want to type. Pls see attached.

X

IVAN

As if taking up a local souse on his fourth-pint challenge, I donned my trainers and a puffy winter coat and headed off through the wind to St. Govan's chapel just before sunset. The 'chapel' is in fact a massive fissure carved into the cliff face containing a crude, stone-built her-

mitage. Legend has it that St. Govan, an Irish monk, made his abode here in the 6th century; trading the psalter for an iPhone, I took his place and kept vigil from dusk 'til dawn.

I saw no floating ladies but got quite a start around 4 AM when, after nodding off before the stone altar inside the hermitage, I awoke to a sound not unlike the peal of a bell. I snatched my phone and ran out into the howling wind (which, unfortunately, overwhelmed my poor micro-phone— the mysterious sound is inaudible). After hearing a series of three peals, I traced the origin back to what locals call the 'bell rock.' Legends of angels sealing a bell inside the stone were undone, unsurprisingly, by what must have been either a result of the wind pounding through the nooks and crannies of the dramatic rock formations or, just as likely, the clank of an unseen yacht anchored off in the fog.

2/20 8:22 AM

Aisha,

I left something out intentionally, didn't seem like good journalism nor does it sound quite right. When I was at the chapel I saw something strange... down on the water, on a patch of moonlight, a shape, black, just about human-sized but too tall by a metre...! I went to get my torch and it was gone when I came back... (are we scared yet?) Sorry to disappoint (i know you want to believe!) but there are markers and buoys all over... and I did have a couple Red Stripes.

x -iv

Pls review conclusion. You know how I work, I have my pudding first;)

Like St. Govan himself, the recent hysteria in Pembrokeshire belongs to the past. Science has kindly relieved us of belief in spirits— we know now that the human 'soul' is only a detail of our material physiology and that evil is a subjective function of an arcane morality. We know enough about our universe to be content in our flesh, doing our best to live and love as good citizens of the planet before we feed the worms.

In that light, it seems ridiculous that a man would spend his prime years here on the edge of the world, locked in combat with both his natural desires and the naturally merciless elements— but when one considers the profound ignorance, corruption, and violence that reigned over St. Govan's Britain, his withdrawal from society becomes almost... rational.

2/21 4:22 PM

Aisha,

So I went to the rocks again last night, I wanted to get a decent field recording of that strange wind effect. This is where it gets dodgy. I'm quite certain I saw that thing again. When I was walking across the peat back to the cottage, it started to smell like roses all about, but there were none... when I looked over my shoulder I got a glimpse of it. It looked like a face, just a bright white face, kind of stood in the dark about 100m behind me out on the peat... mistook it for the moon at first, and couldn't get a photo. Old lady at the cottage says there have been barn owls about. Scared the piss out of me all the same. That face.

Didn't really get any work done today. iv

Never was a place more perfectly suited for the ascetic life; even if there are no angelic bells sealed inside the rocks of this stretch of Welsh coast, there are centuries of lost secrets— and perhaps lost wisdom. Aside from the nagging cold and awesome beauty of the Irish sea, there would be nothing to distract the disciplined monk from the contemplation of his... (what.)

2/21 10:03 PM

Aisha,

I have to admit to you, my dear, that I am absolutely shaking despite myself. The cottage is dark (i swear it got dark at noon today) and i havent had anything to eat. i cant move. the wind (?) is haunting, one can literally hear the banshees. Or banshee, i can say. it sounds like a woman sobbing. for hours. Didn't get anything done today— work is out of the question. Can't sleep. Wish you'd write.

Ivan

2/21 10:31 PM

banshees is Irish roit? what the bloody fuck is she doing in wale

2/21 10:34 PM

I can see her from the window. please don't show this or my drafts to anyone. i don't know

2/22 1:17 AM

aisha she was here in the room with me. Ive seen her face. i dont know what else to say. i cant describe the sorrow. she showed me. that face. he suffered so terribly. oh aisha He suffered so awfully. im going. oh god, oh man

Editors' note: the preceding emails were recorded by the UK's Home Office during their investigation of the incidents reported around Pembrokeshire Coast National Park in Wales earlier this year. On 1 February, three Polish girls reported seeing the figure of a woman standing in the sea off the coast at St. David's Head; subsequently, there have been dozens of reports of mysterious figures, sounds, and solar phenomena. Ivan Rundel, a blogger and writer for the Guardian's Science Weekly, was dispatched to debunk the claims.

The messages were sent from 19 February until just after midnight on the 22nd, when

Rundel was first reported missing. He has not been found. The emails' recipient's name has been changed.

The Mechanics

Joe Hertel

Hello, the sun will not appear today... Hello?"

Odd, there was no response.

Gree checked the communication relays and found them active.

"Hello? Are you receiving?"

"Hey, Gree'tal send your father down the belt, there seems to be a problem with the communication device."

"Very well, Grampa."

"Pops. Hey, Pops."

Grumbling about being disturbed Talgree popped the button and said, "You know I'm busy."

"Sorry, Pops. Grampa needs you at Dawn Horizon."

Talgree hadn't been to Dawn Horizon in hundreds of years. Last time was for an inspection, and another wasn't due for 837 years.

"All right, I'll get on the belt."

"Sorry Pops, that won't work. Had a breakdown at the 6 hour marker."

What? There hadn't been a breakdown in over 10,000 years.

"Has Grampa made the call?"

"Don't think so, said he was having a problem with the communication device."

"Okay, on my way."

He climbed into the cycle and was soon traveling at a top speed of 1,987 miles per hour, only 3 hours to the 6 hour marker. He plugged into the solar system mainframe to access service records, passing the time. The system had come online 157,163 years ago and there had been 17 breakdowns since system inception, but none for 10,326 years. Topsiders had returned to building products of exceptional quality and this system had an expected lifespan of 500,000 years. Hopefully they could return the sun to its half orbit and only miss one day. The last breakdown had taken 3 days and 15 topside engineers to repair.

Clicking the transport communicator he said, "Gree'tal, what is the nature of the breakdown?"

"Guessing its tectonic, Pop."

Humph, "Okay, be there in a couple of hours."

As fifth generation and current catcher Talgree was in charge of the system and responsible for its continual consistent operation. Without information on the problem and an estimated time of repair he could expect topside communication as soon as he arrived at Dawn Horizon. Only two nodes of communication existed to the topside of the planet, one at Dawn Horizon and the other at Dusk Horizon. The planet had stopped revolving well before system inception and way before Talgree's memory.

"Ingenious system," thought Talgree, using old abandoned space elevators to fashion a whip, tipped with a Dyson Sphere to capture the sun each day, harness all of its energy, then whip it back around topside keeping the planet revolving.

Talgree arrived at the 6 hour marker finding Gree'tal measuring the gap between two belts. The belts were a magnetic levitation conveyer system that normally ran at 512 miles per hour, but when a gap of more than 12 feet 3 inches was detected the belt behind the gap would slowly come to a halt.

"Where is the sun?" asked Talgree.

"About 4 miles back."

"How large is the gap?"

"13 feet, 7 inches."

"What was it yesterday?"

"12 feet exactly."

"Metal fatigue?"

"Not that I can detect, Pops."

Almost 5,000 years ago Talgree had given up on getting Gree'tal to stop calling him Pops. Gree'tal was sixth and final generation and some topside engineer probably thought it was funny to give him a teenager's lingo.

"Any issues with the whip link?" asked Talgree.

"Nope, was routine until I felt the safety engage."

1 foot 4 inches was not going to be reduced with all the grease they could find. "All right, going on down to Dawn Horizon for help." said Talgree.

Climbing back into the cycle Talgree clicked on the transport communicator. "Grampa, we've got a gap that's too large to continue Hyperion's race."

"Still no response from topside," said Gree.

"Okay, on my way. Somebody should be there by the time I arrive."

It would take about 2.4 hours using the additional 512 miles per hour from the belt that was still functioning. Talgree ran the cycle up a service ramp onto the belt and was quickly at maximum velocity.

"Puzzling," thought Talgree, topside response should have been established by now. In less than 3 hours the sun will not appear and they'll have no choice but to respond. Plugging back into the mainframe Talgree looked up the last topside communication contact, it had been 737 years ago for a 3 minute delay due to the catch being slowed by solar flares. Talgree shook

his right grabber remembering the additional surge of energy coming from the flares. The energy storage batteries had to be vented that day as they had filled up to capacity from the flare.

Mechanics couldn't really enjoy their jobs, but Talgree had gotten to look forward to the catch. Engaging the crane, tightening the whip, targeting the star, flinging the whip and then closing the massive Dyson sphere around the sun had become an efficient process that he was proud of. At first it took him almost 5 hours to complete the catch, but now he could accomplish his task in under 3 hours. First and second generation took closer to 12 hours to make the catch, so topsiders only got the sun once every two days. Battery storage was not as big back then either, topside had to really scramble to use up all their allotted energy. Now the energy consumption and the energy produced were balanced so that each day the catch, the transport and the throw used up exactly what it produced.

"What do they do with the energy produced topside," wondered Talgree, he had never been topside, built strictly to work on the downside in darkness. His builders had never found a need to provide him with sight sensors, all his work was performed with a laser guidance system. Grampa Gree had ocular circuits but he was not a mobile mechanic, only occupying his throwing shed, never needing to go any place else.

"No response, Son," said Gree greeting Talgree at Dawn Horizon.

"Wow, only three minutes until the sun should rise, you'd think they'd want to know why," stated Talgree.

"We are a mostly forgotten system, Tal, you know that."

"Well, we have earned our reputation for being reliable."

"Grampa, the gap has widened to 14 feet 8 inches, definitely tectonic I felt the rumble," interrupted Gree'tal.

"Check the whip," responded Gree.

"Okay"

"Hello, hello, the sun will not appear today," said Gree into the topside communicator.

"No response in over 5 hours... Odd, they change shifts every 4 hours, so at least 2 topsiders heard the communication," said Talgree.

"Better go check the lines, Son."

Both of the Horizons were hard wired to topside stations as a failsafe for communication. Talgree stepped out of the shed, felt for the communication wire and set out to ensure it was still connected. Only 26 feet from the throwing shed was the topside viewing platform, in the early days of the system Talgree had been told that many Topsiders crowded the platform to see the sun being thrown back into its half orbit. Now, no one watched, no one cared, the sun almost always came up. The line was secure and intact, Talgree popped his communicator switch, "Physical connection confirmed."

"Hello, hello, the sun will not appear today," said Gree.

Talgree waited 5 minutes.

"No response, Tal."

"I heard the message from their loud speakers, how can there be no response?"

Fourth generation and above mechanics were built with the ability to modify their programming, Talgree had built himself worry circuits in an attempt to foresee problems. Gree and Gree'tal had adopted worry circuits as they had become useful in maintaining consistent system service. Now his worry circuits were firing off rapid messages that something was severely wrong.

"Never been past the viewing platform, Gramps, going on over to the control booth."

"Okay," said Gree with a worried edge in his voice.

5 feet from the viewing platform Talgree found the connection line and followed it hoping to find the booth. He found the booth 306 feet from the viewing platform.

"Hello?"

No response.

"Hello!"

"No one here, Gramps. How can that be?"

"Hold on, Son. I'll have to look up protocol."

17 minutes later Gree clicked on, "Can you get in to the booth, Son?

"Sorry, no schematics."

"Sending," responded Gree.

Talgree could suddenly call up what a booth was and found an entryway called "Door". Moving to the door he found that he had to turn a "Doorknob" to gain access, doing so he entered the booth, popped his communicator button and said, "Access accomplished."

"Okay, find the communicator switch."

Using the downloaded schematic his laser system quickly found the switch and in trying to flip it he found some sticks in the way. Brushing them aside he flipped the switch and heard through the communication system, "Response Active."

"Bunch of sticks were in the way, Grampa, but the system is still working."

"Son, turn on the cameras."

Finding the switch cluttered by more sticks Talgree had to remove them to access the cameras.

"OH NO!" Yelled Gree.

"What?"

"Those aren't sticks, they're bones, I can see a hat on one of them. The read out above your head reads 'System Shut Down.'"

"When?"

"737 years ago."

Topsiders had ceased to exist.

One's
Moon

Zara Kand

S he smiled as turquoise jewels glistened in her eyes. Hovering across from her was her Moon, gazing down in all its amorous radiance.

"The wind is picking up," she shuddered, strands of hair waved in the soft glow.

"Come, let's go to bed, I'll keep you warm," crooned the Moon.

She gathered her quilt and smoothed it over the flat boulder, where upon they slept each night. Before climbing up on it, she walked over to their little water fountain and knelt beside it.

"Can we, before we call it a night?" she chirped out into the silent desert air. Grinning, the Moon hovered slightly over and placed its face so that its reflection perfectly haloed that of hers. It was a favorite game of theirs, merging their faces into one glistening sphere upon the water's surface, a playful symbol of their unity. They reveled in this for a moment, and then she felt the warm arms of light luring her onto their rock bed.

"All right, you," she chuckled, "*This* is really our favorite part of night." She curled up onto it.

"That it is." The Moon watched as she unraveled her simple gown, exposing soft, bare skin. Once she had lain down comfortably on her side, it leaned in and caressed her shoulder, hip, legs with its fervent turquoise hue, until her

whole body became illuminated. She let out a soft moan, felt as if she were melting into the sky and ground, and that no boundaries existed between them.

"I love you. I couldn't be any happier than I am right here with you."

"Me too."

She felt the first wave of half-dreams pass over her, but before fully claimed, she caught sight of the metallic sparkles off in the distant landscape, dancing fuzzily, through the slivers of her eyes. She sighed and fell into deep sleep.

The Moon hovered calmly, gazing intently over her, as usual. *My tender young companion,* it thought. *I must remain protective over her, the world can be such an insidious place. Still, in all her naivety, she inspires in me faith that this earthly world harbors much beauty.*

It too suddenly caught sight of the glimmer of those shiny, unnatural looking objects in the distance, and grimaced in disdain. *We have our own paradise here, no need to be burdened by all that crawls out there.*

She awoke, feeling delicious in the morning sun. Her companion had returned to its dim, distant nook in the daytime sky, as it was obliged to until each night fall, but its sultry internal light still lingered within her. She looked upward towards its direction and blew a kiss, and in turn she could see a tiny blink of light beacon back at her. She lowered herself from the rock and began her normal routine of tidying up the perimeter of their dwelling. Restoring all its arrangements each morning after the wind's toil was quite a task, yet also something to pass the time until her Moon's return. Simple and satisfying was their home; a few logs for sitting, a fire pit for cooking, a fountain for washing, and a flat rock for sleeping. *So many joyous nights have been had here*, she thought. *In depth conversations about life, songs sung, star gazing, light-making, fantastic dreaming…*

After sweeping away layers of dust, she noticed some of her garments had blown out past some nearby rocks and clung to a few scraggly juniper trees. As she went to retrieve the garments, she again noticed those unnatural twinkles in the distance, curiosity rousing her slightly. Instantly she clutched at the vial that hung from her neck. It was a special gift from her companion; inside shined a concentrated amount of the Moon's very own essence, a symbol of sacrifice and of its loving presence, even when afar.

It had warned her about such foreign objects which appeared real and inviting, yet whose only intent is to stray one from their natural path. *If over there exist things that are irrelevant to real life, then it should be of no consequence that I go simply as an observer. I'm mature enough to make my own mind up about such matters,* she thought. In one impulsive instant she resolved to set foot upon territory which she had vowed so many times never to do. Her first timid steps forward gradually accelerated into an eager stride, while her vial necklace delicately dangled from her chest. She passed through familiar trails and various rock formations, occasionally looking behind her shoulder at their humble dwelling, becoming smaller and smaller until it was but a speck in the desert haze.

Suddenly she reached a part of the land in which there was a noticeable shift in the ground, its texture softer and of a reddish color. She had made it to the outskirts of her familiar territory. And there, about four feet before her, sat one of those shiny metallic objects, which had aroused her curiosity so and led her to this foreign place. It was a two inch trapezoid which at first appeared static. As though sensing her attention, it suddenly sprung into an insect-like configuration, spiny legs shot outward and a beaded head emerged. Startled, she took a step back, to which it reciprocated a bashful stance and they stood gazing at one another. Its shiny eyes were captivating, and she then felt herself drawn closer. It began making endearing, theatrical motions with its legs, as if for her benefit, and she smiled and put out her hand. It leapt up and caressed her palm. As soon as it sensed relaxation from her, the creature once again reconfigured itself into the flat trapezoid that it had been previously. However, rather than refract the sun's light as any solid object, it seemed to display a sort of inward screen, as if a window into another realm. She lost all sense of her surroundings and stared into this cloudy, tiny window.

She saw flashes of villages, parades being held... Cheering crowds gathered around what seemed persons of nobility. The window zoomed in to make out the detail of what was the center of interest, which in each scene appeared to be a single female, adorned with satiny robe and seductive jewels, flamboyant head piece made of phosphorescent, alternating colors. Bystanders were clearly ravished by the presence of each one of these goddesses, who in turn devoured their adoration, flashing an impersonal wink or smile occasionally. *They look so elegant... so superior,* she thought. For the first time in her life she felt a tinge of envy, made aware of her humble get up and beginning to feel as though it no longer sufficed.

This sudden sensation of hers served as the object's definitive cue. It instantaneously jumped from her hand and dug itself into her cloth gown.

Mouth agape, she peered down at the object attached to her navel. It was now reconfigured into an oval shape, similar to that of the jewels worn by the admired, only larger. She couldn't deny it was a beautiful addition to her get up. She did a twirl in the breeze, admiring her new adornment. She felt hungry for more, wanted more beauty. It so happened that every few feet popped up more metallic objects, offering themselves to her by way of the same ceremony; alluring her with windows into other tantalizing realms, and then attaching themselves to her gown.

While this activity ensued, the Moon watched from above with disappointment. *Doesn't she know how beautiful she is, internally radiant, without needing the external help of these devious little creatures?*

With each new oval jewel she grew heavier, but her vanity high made her feel light as a feather. So absorbed was she in her new additions that she didn't notice the several times her beloved Moon had twinkled light in her direction. She began imagining herself applauded by large covetous crowds, carried away to distant lands where monuments boasted her form and servants bled for her.

She came upon a little oasis in which a clear glaze of water beckoned her forth. Her growing thirst in the desert heat overlooked, she instead found herself captivated by the exquisite reflection staring back at her. Flaunting smiles and angling the jewels so that they sparkled at the water's surface, it began to bubble. Gradually the water rose to her eye level and split into two liquid bodies. They were both nearly identical, dashing female forms, and very familiar to her.

"Who are you two?" she asked in amazement. They laughed mischievously.

"You could say that we are your sisters… In one way or another." They began dancing seductively and pulled her into their circular vortex. Laughter, hair and beads of water flung about in spiraling frenzy. Under the delirium, she was aware of losing herself completely to these dazzling forms, and she surrendered, carelessly. They swirled her about, their eyes hungry upon her.

"Give me your jewels," said one, "I am not beautiful enough." Without hesitation she twisted the oval jewels from her gown and flung them into the belly of the water being. "Now I have almost enough to be loved."

The other water body came to embrace her, demanding, "Give me your vial. I am so beautiful, that I deserve to be loved by all." The being shined an irresistible smile into her. Overtaken,

she untied the vial necklace and handed it over
without further thought. Far off in the distant sky,
a speck of light showed a degree dimmer.

"You have nothing further to offer us." came
a cold chorus, and with this their forms descen-
ded as a spiraling mass back into the flat of the
water's surface, without a trace. All the exciting
commotion ended so abruptly as if she had just
woken from a disturbing dream. Breathless and
nearly paralyzed, she collapsed to the ground.
She felt hollow, as if something terrible had just
happened.

There in the late evening sun, she fell asleep
hard at the water's edge. The scent of her tired,
tender skin carried into the air and roused the attention of the nearby desert vermin, awakening
from their unsuspected nests. They crept out,
found her laying there and one by one planted
little teeth marks into her pale, limp body.

She awoke to the setting sun and its accom-
panying brilliant red smeared across the horizon
in violent patches. She shook her head in disori-
entation, the previous day's events came flooding
back to her. *My Vial!* She reached at her vacant
chest with dread, also noticing pangs of pain
shooting throughout her body. She looked down
at dozens of oozing red holes, to which slender
trails of blood snaked down her limbs and into

the water, where it dissipated into a murky red reflection. She began to cry.

In this combination of water, blood and tears she stared at her face in misery, wishing desperately for her companion to return as it normally did this time of evening. The sun had long since reclined into the hills and the smears of red had been replaced by a tranquil blue black sky. Then finally, after many quiet, ruthless hours, she felt her skin begin to tingle. Like a graceful phantom across this blue black reflection came gliding in a brilliant, milky turquoise sphere and landed in place behind her face, creating a soft halo.

"You fool of mine," said the Moon endearingly, "Don't you know that I live for you, revolve just to see you smile each day?"

"I know," she managed a smile between weeping, "I have given something sacred away. I believe I have some work to do, to give back what was lost. Come, let us take rest upon our rock bed, I will shine onto you all the light I have, the kind that can't be taken away."

They returned to their humble dwelling, within which all the true riches in the world are sought.

Katie of
the Stars

Robert DeLoyd

"Katie, come quick I need you in engineering," called Jason over her com.

"I heard the Captain wants to see you at your convenience," said Nell peeking her head into Katie's cabin.

"I just got a call from Jason, he wants me down in engineering. His voice sounded urgent too."

"You still read those printed books?" Nell asked as Katie was getting out of her bunk.

"I wish!" she replied as the hologram of *The One Hundred and One Dalmatians* by Dodie Smith vanished from her hands to appear back on the shelf next to a long row of her tech manuals and a couple of her favorites; *A Little Princess* and *The Secret Garden* by Frances Hodgson Burnett. "Nothing takes the place of real paper," continued Katie, "but this will have to do. Tell the Captain I'll be on the bridge as soon as I find out what trouble Jason got himself..."

She didn't get to finish the last part of her sentence as the lights flashed in her room and down the corridor and a sudden sense of weightlessness was felt. Items not secured were floating for a few brief seconds and then, Wham! Katie and Nell were hit by heavy gravity that put

Nell lying flat on the corridor deck and Katie back in her bed. Klaxons were sounding all over the ship.

"Damn, we hard dropped out of warp!" Katie shouted and waited in bed a few seconds to make sure it didn't happen again.

She went over to Nell to help her up on her feet, "You okay, Nell?"

"I'll be fine. You best get your butt over to engineering to find out what's going on."

Jumping over and maneuvering her way around other fallen crew members, she ran down the corridors as fast as she could to engineering. When she passed sickbay, she noticed crew members were already being treated. One walked out with an arm in a sling and Katie almost collided with her, just bumping her a bit, "Sorry," is all she said to the woman as she ran on towards her destination.

The elevators weren't functioning and hubots were working to free those of the crew stuck inside. She'd have to take the stairs down four levels which would delay her, so she took the nearest trash chute and slid down to land hard on her butt in a dumpster on the lowest level where the engine room and warpdrive resided. She climbed out of the dumpster wiping something looking like spaghetti off her work fatigues as she walked the few yards to the engine room.

Once inside she saw Jason lying on the floor not moving. She kneeled over checking for a pulse and seeing if he was breathing; he was out cold and she called for a medic. She quickly made Jason comfortable and treated him for shock, then headed for the warpdrive to give it the once over.

Stepping up to the control console Katie noticed the red lights flashing to the drive's four cooling systems, one for each Higgs Injector, warning that the whole drive was overheating and if something wasn't done shortly the injectors would meltdown and form a virtual mini black hole inside the ship. This would be none too good for the ship and those inside.

The injectors create a mini black hole out of virtual particles by projecting Higgs Bosons to a fine point out in front of the ship. As the ship gains speed, the hole is projected along, causing the ship and everything close by to fall faster towards the hole. Once the ship and the hole are manipulated close enough it creates a warpfield as it nears, but never reaches the event horizon surrounding the hole. This virtual mini black hole can be shut down when the ship reaches its destination.

She began the procedure of cutting the flow of the Higgs field to each injector. Sweat dripped off her brow as Katie turned the dials and watched the four gauge needles climb deeper into the critical red zone. She persisted even though the situation looked hopeless because the drive was now pulsing a hot orange. Little by little all four gauge needles dropped down from critical to normal. She quickly vented the drive to space. It would take a few hours to cool enough to have a look inside. After this was done she had to divert all energy to the life support and mission critical systems; meaning the ship was dead in the water, the proper euphemism Katie thought.

Standing in the engine bay behind Katie was the Captain and a few of the bridge crew intently watching her move around the machinery, trying not to disturb her until she completed her task of safely bringing the drive back from critical. They were all aware of what would happen if she was distracted and the drive blew.

Finally, the job was done and Katie turned around to go sit and wait for the drive to cool down.

"Report!" commanded the Captain, relieved the ship and crew didn't implode.

"The injectors are clogged, Captain," Katie replied quickly in one breath, considering the Captain already knew how a warpdrive works.

"How long until the drive is operational?" asked the Captain.

"That depends on what I find when I inspect the insides of the drive, once it cools down. I believe I can give you a better idea after this is done."

"Okay, carry on," said the Captain and turned to leave, but then stopped to add, "and thanks for bringing the drive down safely."

"Yes, Ma'am!" Katie proudly replied to her Captain.

After two hours of cooling the drive was safe to enter. Katie unbolted the heavily armored service hatch and shimmied on through with her test equipment. Once inside she could walk around and inspect the massive injectors protruding from the walls of the ship's engine room. She began with the basic maintenance checklist, examining and probing for fractures or flaws; the integrity of the drive. She did this first, because if she found anything wrong at this point, it would be useless to go any farther until repairs were made. A good hour went by and she found nothing suspect. Now she went for the injector heads themselves to see what was causing them to clog.

She climbed up the scaffolding of the closest injector and cranked down the metal walkway leading to the injector head. Katie didn't see anything at first, then just a blur surrounding the

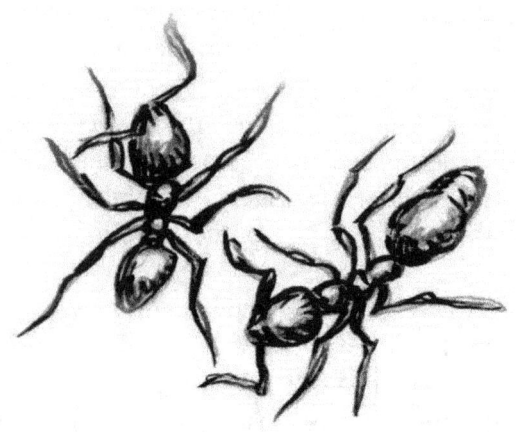

head. She flipped down her magnifying glasses and set them for infrared vision. What she saw astounded her... Multidimensional space ants phasing in and out of realities, must have been drawn to the Higgs Injectors, clogging them up. She had heard stories of these tiny creatures; hundreds of them can fit on the surface of a tablespoon and not be noticed.

She called the Captain, "Ma'am, the injectors are clogged by space ants."

"We must have picked them up on Orion station. Probably on our last visit there. The whole ship must be infested with the dang things. I'll have the hubots start sanitizing and flushing them out into space."

"Captain, I always thought these ants were fiction, a fairytale told by old spacefaring crew to scare the newbies," inquired Katie.

"I'll send a team down there to exterminate them for you. You just keep working and get our drive back up and running. None Such Ideas Dissipate…"

"Pardon me, Ma'am?"

"It essentially means anything is possible until it slips your mind."

Your Honor and 'His Likeness'

Gabriel Hart

Like (lik) *adjective.* (of a portrait or other image) having a faithful resemblance to the original.

The mid-afternoon sun shone beamlike through each window on the westside of the courtroom. The figurative dust had settled after a longer than normal recess, save a few clearing of throats from the jury. The judge shuffled his papers and adjusted his glasses until the room came into focus, then looked at his papers while moving them to the tip of his nose.

"Mr. Barnes, would you come to the stand."

The judge spoke commandingly under his breath with almost no indication that it was a question. Mr. Barnes had already gotten up out of his seat with the mere mention of his name, eagerly anticipating his summoning.

"Your Honor, I found the iPhone belonging to my best friend, Jason Krieger. He had been missing for almost a week back in January, until I went looking for him and found his phone across the street from his house at the end of a vacant lot. Everything that makes him who he is is on this phone – his voice, his image, his friends and loved ones, his interests and burdens... so we can essentially consider it "his likeness" – as if he is here with us on the stand. Let me know if this sounds weird to you."

Mr. Barnes paused, anticipating a response from the stoic judge.

"I should also say that he was a writer… I'm sorry, IS a writer and musician, and that he was always full of ideas that he would record into his phone, just to give some context."

The judge puckered approvingly and nodded his head.

"Okay, here it is… The subject is 'Chris Issak,' This recording is named, from what I can gather, after a song idea that may have stylistically reminded him of that contemporary singer/songwriter."

"La, la, la, la, LA, la la…

La, la, la, la, la, la, la, la, la, la, la"

"Then there is this other recording, just seconds after which reads: Guitar part, Chris Issakey."

"Der, der, der, der der, der, dow, dow, der, der, dow."

"Sorry… let me skip ahead… but then he starts saying all this."

"I hoped you liked that. Whoever I'm talking to. HA! Anyway, I am standing here in my drive-way of tiny stones, it's all gravel. The gavel that the judge pounds down. But I am the wood on

wood on wood on wood, so let the judge and the jury pound the fuck down!"

The courtroom stirred with muted giggles and a confused restlessness. Was this a joke?

"Uh... sorry, your Honor. I forgot that some of this was on there. I honestly don't know what he was talking about there... he tends to get carried away, but just bear with me here. And on the same note, I'll go ahead and warn you, and the jury, that there's a liberal helping of expletives contained herein.

"That's fine. Proceed, please."

"So, then there's this."

"But okay... I'm standing here, right in my driveway, and I'm hearing this sound."

(pause)

"It, it sounds like a child... like a crying child?"

(rearranging, clacking...)

"Trying to pick it up, here... It's so fucking eerie and it's so quiet out here, so I don't want to get too close to where anyone can hear me, in case there really is something weird going on."

(whispering)

"I swear to God it sounds like a child across the street, but I'm positive they don't have any kids... Like a child in some kind of pain?

"Ok, so let me fill in some blanks here for

posterity... I live in this place called Morongo Valley. I moved here a little over a year ago, and with what I gather, including me, it seems like everybody that lives here moved here to get away from something...

"*All my neighbors are kinda weird. The ones you see, anyway. I can go weeks without seeing any of 'em. The ones I have seem like old, defeated shut-ins. Definitely no one under the age of 50 or 60, mostly single. Definitely no children anywhere, probably for miles. Oh, and do yourself a favor and DO NOT go on one of those sex offender websites for this area. You're not gonna like what you see. But I guess it would make sense for a convicted chi-mo to move here for some peace and lack of temptation...*

"*Ok, I'm moving closer... Walking tip-toe across the street. Ok, THERE! I hope this is picking it up, this is one of the fucking strangest things I've ever heard... I'll shut up for a sec here...*"

As Mr. Barnes held his friend up to the mic, a mournful, disarming cry filled the courtroom, its ambience cloaking every member of the jury spellbound. Many of their mouths slowly opened, chillingly, as if they were the ones making the noise. The judge, too, was just as taken aback, as he surveyed the jury's reaction. The palpable impact it was having on his jury was frightening him, nearly making him lose his composure... as if they had all heard this sound before but had spent a lifetime suppressing the memory, until this unfortunate moment.

"Will you please turn the phone off, Mr. Barnes?"

"Your Honor, but this is where it escalates..."

"PLEASE TURN THE PHONE OFF OR I WILL HOLD YOU IN CONTEMPT OF COURT!"

Mr. Barnes startlingly turned the recording off, still looking at his friend: the phone, in defeat.

"We are going to take a brief recess and return in twenty minutes." said the judge, as he smoothed out every non-existent wrinkle in his robe.

———●———

During the break there arose a theory, though unspoken by everyone, even by the judge (who sat by himself with his eyes closed for the duration), that could easily explain the sound away as one of Jason Krieger's neighbors, somehow all of a sudden having a baby in their house for no good reason, it being left to cry in front of a window fan, as the wail had a sort of tremolo effect, its characteristics almost digital and lending to something human but laced something wholly un-organic. But the logistics of this theory came more from an element of absolute panic, an emergency go-to fire-escape in the architecture of the mind, keeping us from the inherent danger of reality. It is often that one may seek a support group of others to help perpetuate a falsehood that they know in their own soul not to be 100% true, and it's with this very "strength in numbers" that we give weight to not just certain philosophies, but most occurrences that we have not experienced firsthand. The judge and jury in this case had found themselves sandwiched between a double-layer of their own deceit, as it was clear Jason's phenomena was having the same triggered emotional recall within them all, just not the actual memory to serve it with any legal validity. So, they just made shit up to further suppress a memory within them all that there may have been convenient words for in a psychologist's office, though not in the nature of a courtroom where it's needed most at this near-boiling moment.

The jury filed back into the courtroom and the judge took his seat, as well as Mr. Barnes. The judge cleared his throat and spoke.

"Mr. Barnes, can you go ahead and finish playing Mr. Krieger's recording, right where we left off?"

With the phone already in his hand, he tapped the screen.

"Okay so in case it doesn't come out fully audible here, I'm going to get even closer. I'm pretty sure it's coming from the backroom of my neighbor's place... There's a little vacant lot here on the side, so I shouldn't be too obvious..."

There was the brief crunch of Jason's cowboy boots on his neighbor's gravel landscaping, then more silent pats once he was on the dirt of the vacant lot, traveling alongside the one-story home.

"Fuck. It's so loud now..."

The jurors returned to their previous emotional state, but more so... Transfixed, wanting for more to be revealed, so it could finally stop, but also wanting it to stop immediately. As if there was a volume switch being slowly turned up that was connected to their full spectrum of possible response and hybrid emotions there were not yet words for. Mr. Barnes looked up to see the judge's head downcast with his eyes closed, again.

"Okay, now this is weird… It's definitely not coming from the neighbors. I'm in the vacant lot, now past their place and as I walk farther past and I can hear it louder…"

(sounds of leaves brushing, twigs snapping)

"I'm like, twelve meters beyond the neighbor's house now, I don't know, it's dark as fuck and I'm just advancing into more darkness and small branches keep whacking me in the face and I'm praying there's no cactus or cholla over here and I'm freaking out cause now it sounds like its right fucking here…

"Oh my, God…

"Oh my fucking, fucking, God…"

From there, his voice on the recording gets extremely muffled and it sounds like he is scrambling with his phone. But Jason was saying something important, over and over, in the same rhythm and inflection, then quickly returns to audible comprehension.

"I knew it! I fucking knew it! This is fucking incredible…"

Jason's voice had gone from whispers of desperate fear to absolute ecstasy and a hush of relief – though more confusion – wafted across the jury.

Mr. Barnes spoke, "Your Honor, that is all that is there. I have not been able to make out that muffled part before he…"

"Well, it sounded to me like he said something like 'photo,' like he was obviously going to take a goddamn photo, for Christ-sake!" the judge interrupted, finally losing his professionalism to his passion.

Mr. Barnes shook his head, embarrassed with epiphany and thankful for the judges sharp ears.

"Of course... Jesus Christ. Of course. I cannot believe I didn't think of that..."

Barnes dove into the phone with both hands, tapping the screen until the photo icon revealed Jason's cache of memories, and tapped hard and triumphant on the last one.

"Good fucking LORD!"

Barnes zoomed on the photo with his thumb and forefinger.

"Your Honor, I can't believe what I am looking at with my own eyes. Since your senses are clearly sharper than mine, please have a look at this," he said as he stood up and held out the phone to the judge.

The judge eagerly outstretched his hand where it momentarily hung for humble deliverance, much like a religious painting. He swiftly brought it into his chest and threw his head down to view, almost miserly, as tears welled up behind his bifocals.

Through his fully erupting sobbing he could barely make out the command to break for recess, but the jury understood and began to leave their seats.

For his last memory as a human on this Earth, Jason Krieger encountered a "child of the sky." A baby, but not like ours. Naked, the photo saw it to have no genitalia and its eyes, vertical ovals that took up large residence on its otherwise human-esque face.

Its cries were not borne of physical pain, but of abandonment. Its "family" banishing it to

Earth to be among the loneliest creatures in the Universe, those who would also never quite measure up to the standards of their far more advanced world. The Earth was their trashcan, or at best, their convenient Purgatory of Imperfection. But in an apparently universal "take one, leave one" gesture, the beings of the sky would initially plan their descent to take Jason Krieger, who's vivid, sweeping imagination made his head already that much "in the clouds" making him an obvious choice for "psychic harvesting" their planet's main industry and export.

But we are blessed to still have his likeness here on Earth. Jason Krieger was the first to become a phone.

Now, we are all phones.

Like.

A Hard Day Hunting Dinosaurs

Brent A. Harris

The creature, quick and birdlike, darted beneath the underbrush. My eyes swept towards it. I took a restrained step closer. Even as a juvenile, my prey was lethal. Just under waist high, flat brown and green mottled feathers blended in and around the bushes and foliage of the late Mesozoic. A perfect camouflage.

My eyes trained forward, not looking for my prey but eliminating where it *wasn't*. While this was my first-time hunting Tyrannosaur, it wasn't my first-time hunting dinosaurs. I'd tired of setting lazy traps for Triceratops and snares for Stegos. I'd chased down the faster ostrich-like creatures and outwitted packs of raptors – movies made them out to be far more fearsome than the overgrown turkeys they turned out to be. In fact, most of the ones I'd brought back to Earth Prime were no bigger than the young Tyrannosaur I was currently tracking. A disappointment to say the least. I wanted something *bigger.*

Oh well. I'd bag this one, head back to my beat-up transport truck. Punch in the dial for my return trip home, and try another Mesozoic-era Earth in the morning. Dinosaur hunting wasn't as lucrative as it used to be. Too many of us out here doing it now. Most folks back on Earth Prime could order a Bronto-burger at their local drive-thru. But it paid the bills, and it was inter-

esting Earth-hopping, seeing all these other Earths in their infancy. We could do whatever we wanted to them. It wasn't going to mess with our timeline.

The juvenile Tyrannosaur let out a noise somewhere between a choked chirp and a roar. I suppose it was transitioning from weening off its mom to learning how to be a little dinosaur. But it must have gotten caught in something, because those stumbling cries sounded like the creature was in distress. It needed help. Luckily, I was there.

The Rex's calls lured me on, beckoning me closer. Brushing branches from my face, I followed the pleas into the foliage. She was laying on her side, entangled in roots and branches, feathers flapping wildly. Females had almost no color to them. And they were larger, fiercer than their male counterparts. She ripped and tore at her bindings. I almost felt bad as I raised my rifle and prepared to call it in. Dinosaurs required special transports. I thought better of it; the cost was prohibitive. It bit into my profits, leaving me with even little after the taxes for time-travel and Earth-hopping. It's hard making an honest living. I thought I could probably jam this juvenile into my transport and save a few credits.

I probably should have kept a closer eye on my surroundings. I was tired and distracted. It'd been a long day and I wanted to go home, crash on the couch, and watch my hometown ball players give lessons on how to lose badly. It was the smell of decomposing meat that made me question where I was. At first, I thought it might mean we were near the little creature's nest. That made sense. She sensed danger and was running home to mommy.

No. If I was near the nest, the smell would permeate the air with a sickly, sweet aroma of raw meat and decaying flesh. Instead, the foulness came in waves, hot and sticky. The branches were still except for where the juvenile thrashed about. There was no wind.

The creature settled down and hopped easily and effortlessly out from the tangle of plants and then scooted away. Not a feather was ruffled. *The little bastard tricked me.*

It turned out I wasn't the only hunter here. I hit my emergency button as hard and as quick as I could and breathed a sigh of relief when I felt the reassuring buzz signaling that the message had been sent.

My message would go back to Earth Prime, and a team of rescuers would track my location and arrive five minutes before my stupid, stupid mistake to prevent me from making it. Sure, it would cost a fortune, and I'd have to pull in twice as much for a while to stay afloat, but at least I'd be alive. I wouldn't be watching ballgames anytime soon. I grunted in disproval. It was my own damned fault.

But that timeline didn't exist yet. For now, I'd have to see this one through. The large tyrannosaur poked its pink snout out, exposing teeth long and sharp and jagged enough where I hoped it would be over soon, yet I knew I'd feel everything in the first few terrifying moments until I finally died of shock or exsanguination.

The mother dinosaur had been so still. So peaceful. It was a good arrangement. Let her helpless daughter lure in the food, and then momma would take the prey down. Only, I was the prey and I had fallen right for it. I guess when there are failsafes like time-travel, it tones down the human instinct to survive. There's little need to be careful. *But I should. Oh, I should be very careful next time.* This was going to hurt. This was going to hurt so much.

The tyrannosaur lunged.

AUTHORS

●

JAKES BAYLEY was born in Seattle, WA, and has lived in southern France, London, San Francisco and Los Angeles, where he currently resides. His writing was generally shaped by the physical geography of his native Pacific Northwest, and by the human and spiritual histories of western Europe as they manifest themselves in the churches and architectural ruins of France. Among his literary influences he would count L.F. Céline, D.H. Lawrence, the letters of Simone Weil, Yukio Mishima, Theodore Roethke, Theodor Adorno, Ernst Jünger, and John the Apostle/John of Patmos.

JON CHRISTOPHER was born and raised in Southern California. He lives with his love of more than 30 years, Tania, in the hi-desert overlooking Joshua Tree National Park. Jon's either writing, creating music, painting or designing books for Traveling Shoes Press – and always spending time with Suki the dog. Jon has written four novels, and two have been published; *Some-*

where Out There In The West and *Moving At The Speed of Time*. His third novel, *Meanwhile There Were Dragon*s, is coming out in November, 2018. You can visit his website at:
jonandtania.com

ROBERT DELOYD lived peacefully aboard his 26-foot sailboat on a mooring in Redondo Beach, California for 22 years. He moved to Joshua Tree in 1997 and wrote a small weekly column in the local newspaper for 11 years. Robert is amazed at the life out where he lives, the folks he calls his friends, and is excited to share them with you, even the fictional ones. He has eight Kindle novels, as well as one paperback available on Amazon.com

JEAN-PAUL L. GARNIER lives and writes in Joshua Tree, CA where he is co-owner of *Space Cowboy Books*, a science fiction bookstore, independent publisher, and producer of *Simultaneous Times* podcast. In 2018 Traveling Shoes Press released *Echo of Creation*, a collection of his science fiction short stories. He has also released two collections of poetry: *the Spiraling Pearls* (HD Press 2010) and *In Iudicio* (Cholla Needles Press 2017). His short stories, poetry, and essays have appeared in: *Specklit, Eye to the*

Telescope, Scifaikuest, and many other anthologies and webzines. He holds a certificate in creative writing from Wesleyan University. **jplgarnier.blogspot.com**

BRENT A. HARRIS is a Sidewise Award nominated author of time-travel and alternate history shenanigans. His book, *A Time of Need,* is a retelling of the Revolutionary War with Washington recast as a redcoat. He lives in 29 Palms with his family, where he's lived long enough to become convinced that Joshua Trees, are in fact, real trees. You can find more of his work at **brentaharris.com**

GABRIEL HART lives in Morongo Valley in California's High Desert. He is the ringleader of the L.A. based punk Wall of Sound group Jail Weddings, who just completed work on their third album *Blood Moon Blue.* Their previous album *Meltdown: A Declaration of Unpopular Emotion* (2013) was voted Best Album of The Year by *L.A. Weekly,* followed by Best Band of the Year in 2014. His debut twin novels *Virgins In Reverse / The Intrusion* will be published in 2019. His chapbook *Cinema of Life* (2016) and current novelette *Nothing To See Here* (2017) will be incorporated into his upcoming desert-noir novel *Lies of Heaven*, to be released unabridged by Space Cowboy. His short-fiction and poetry have recently been published in *Cholla Needles, Howl* 2018 Anthology. He is also a regular contributor to *L.A. Record*, a Los Angeles music publication: **gabrielhart.net**

JOE HERTEL grew up behind the perfect curtain of Orange County, with the perfect streets, the clean parks and perfect neighbors. Plenty of room for an imagination to fill in all the rough spots and dream of dark lords in outer space. Over his back fence was one of the last orange orchards left in the city, it was turned into middle earth after school as well as on weekends. The books he read as a child set up a life long love of reading and defined his passion for stories. He now lives in Yucca Valley.

ZARA KAND lives and works in the high desert of California. She spends her time oil painting, illustrating, curating art shows, catering, and running a book store. Every now and then she manages to squeeze a story out of her, when given approval by the literary gods. **zarakand.com**

OTHER TITLES FROM SPACE COWBOY BOOKS

The Third Horseman – Vallejo translations
R. Soos

Adrift
Patti Jeane Pangborn

I'm Sending Messages into Outer Space
Rik Livingston

The Father
Jakes Bayley

Nothing to See Here
Gabriel Hart

Cinema of Life
Gabriel Hart

The Inflatable Catechism
Giovanni Garcia

LGBT+ Voices
Various Poets

World of Sugar
[x-AT]

The Great Encounter
Jean-Paul L. Garnier

Future Anthropology
Jean-Paul L. Garnier

Us, Clone
Jean-Paul L. Garnier

Available at spacecowboybooks.com